fect

To
Lyle, Capri, Sutton & Pa

& Fredrik!

Fredrik *goes to* Hollywood

Piccadil   Productions

LLC

Janet York

J anet and Fredrik felt the Hollywood talent scout's gaze upon them as Fredrik sailed over his first jump, scrambled around the weave poles, and dashed through the tunnel. They'd practiced these agility sequences hundreds of times. The tough course didn't intimidate them. The cheering crowds didn't distract them. They focused on one obstacle at a time. Fredrik had to win. His future depended on it.

Janet held her breath as her little Cavalier flew over his second jump, then scampered up and down the seesaw without faltering. "That's my Angel Boy! Show Mr. Bigalow what you can do."

1

Sit,
Walk Around
Dog

Fredrik triumphed. He scored a personal best and won a blue ribbon.

"You're a great team," Mr. Bigalow said. "Tell me more."

Janet wondered what the Hollywood agent was looking for. "Fredrik's not just another adorable dog. Right now, he's the American Kennel Club's number one Cavalier King Charles Spaniel. Not only has he won several *Best in Shows*, he's a certified pet therapy dog. We visit hospitals and nursing homes. You should see how gentle and loving he is with kids and seniors."

"Impressive!" said Mr. Bigalow. He made notes in his little black book.

"Fredrik's also an advanced rally dog," said Janet. "He's a whiz at hand signals and reads body language to perfection. That's important on a movie set."

"Essential," said Mr. Bigalow, scrutinizing the steadfast little spaniel at his owner's side.

Piccadil Productions Presents
Starring
Janet and Fredrik

Fredrik and the TRAMP

Janet twisted the lead around her hand. "Fredrik's dreamed of being in films ever since he saw *Lady and the Tramp* when he was a pup."

"Really?" Mr. Bigalow made a frame with his thumbs and forefingers centering Fredrik in his view.

"Really!" said Janet. "And he has acting experience. Sometimes we perform skits for seniors in nursing homes."

Fredrik is
Driving
Miss Janet

"We've done *Driving Miss Janet,*
Fredrik Fully Loaded,
Fredrik and the Biscuit Factory,

7

Janet and Fredrik are out of this world!

F.T.
Fredrik Terrestrial

Fredrik Terrestrial, Fredrik's Angels, and *King Fredrik.* That one makes me cry. I can't imagine what I'd do if anything ever happened to my precious Angel Boy."

FREDRIK'S ANGELS

KING FREDRIK

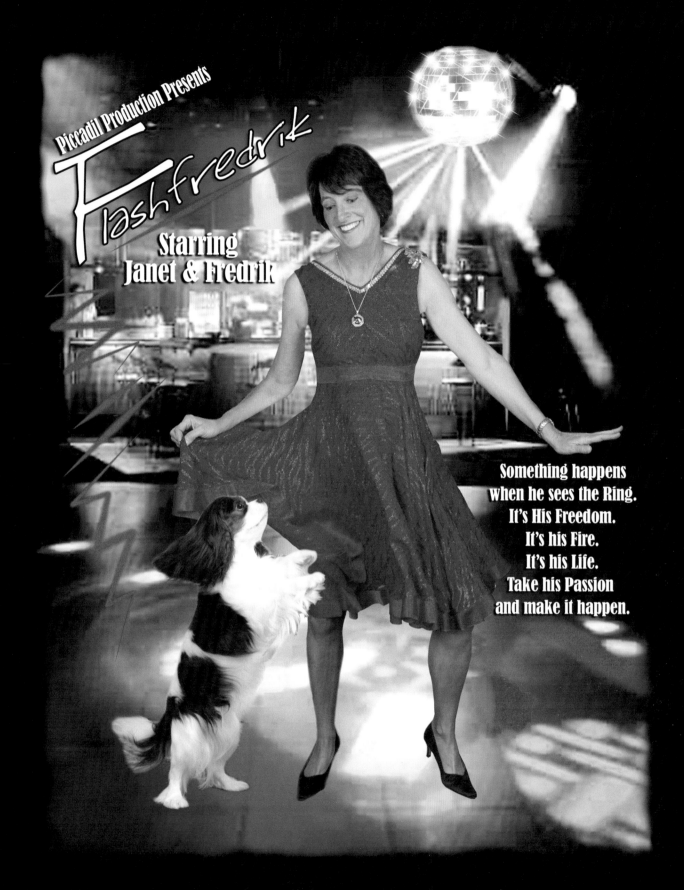

Piccadil Production Presents

Flashfredrik

Starring
Janet & Fredrik

Something happens
when he sees the Ring.
It's His Freedom.
It's his Fire.
It's his Life.
Take his Passion
and make it happen.

"Quite a repertoire," said Mr. Bigalow. "Any other talents?"

"He sings and dances," said Janet. "Fredrik holds a howl longer than an opera star holds a note. And we're into freestyling. When we dance together, they call us Ginger Rogers and Fredrik Astaire."

"You give new meaning to top hat and *tails.*" Mr. Bigalow laughed at his own joke. "Does Fredrik like to travel?"

"He was born in Holland—just like his great-grandfather, Corneel, The Plaza hotel's Young Ambassador," said Janet, "and he's been on the go ever since."

Mr. Bigalow reached down to pet Fredrik. "I might have something for him in LA. They're doing a remake of *The Glorious Adventure.* It's set during the reign of King Charles II at the time of the Great London Fire. They'll probably need several Cavaliers."

Before Janet could tell him about her other special dogs, loud barking interrupted their conversation. A bouncy Golden Retriever in the next ring had knocked over the high bar, picked it up in his mouth, and with tail wagging, dropped it on the judge's foot. The crowd roared with laughter.

"Now *that's* what I'm looking for—*a comedian!*" Mr. Bigalow turned his back on Fredrik and walked away, leaving Janet speechless.

By the end of the day, Fredrik had proven he was *Lord of the Rings*.

One Fredrick
To Rule The Ring

He'd won three more awards: *Best in Breed, Best in Toy Group,* and *Best in Show.* But as the judge handed the special little Cavalier top honors, Mr. Bigalow handed the Golden Retriever's owner a contract.

Janet and Fredrik heard the agent say, "Your dog has an elusive quality—a combination of personality and presence. Sign on the dotted line, and I'll make your Golden a star."

On the ride home to Manhattan, Fredrik curled up in the back of the van with his head between his paws. He'd worked so hard. One by one he'd mastered every obstacle and won every event. He had "personality" and "presence." Why didn't the Hollywood agent pick him?

For weeks after the show, Fredrik moped around the house. Janet cuddled him close and read him stories. When the fragrant roses on their penthouse terrace burst into bloom, she tried to coax him outdoors to play. They took long walks in Central Park. But when they returned, he crawled into his doggie bed and slept.

He didn't exercise on his treadmill. He didn't play "chase" and "tug-of-war" with Paddy, Pippin, Nikkie, and Cecile or "keep-away" with Boogie Woogie Broadway, Mondrian, and the other dogs. Day after day, he watched "Animal Planet" and "Discovery Channel." Nothing perked him up. Not even little Eli's gentle nuzzles.

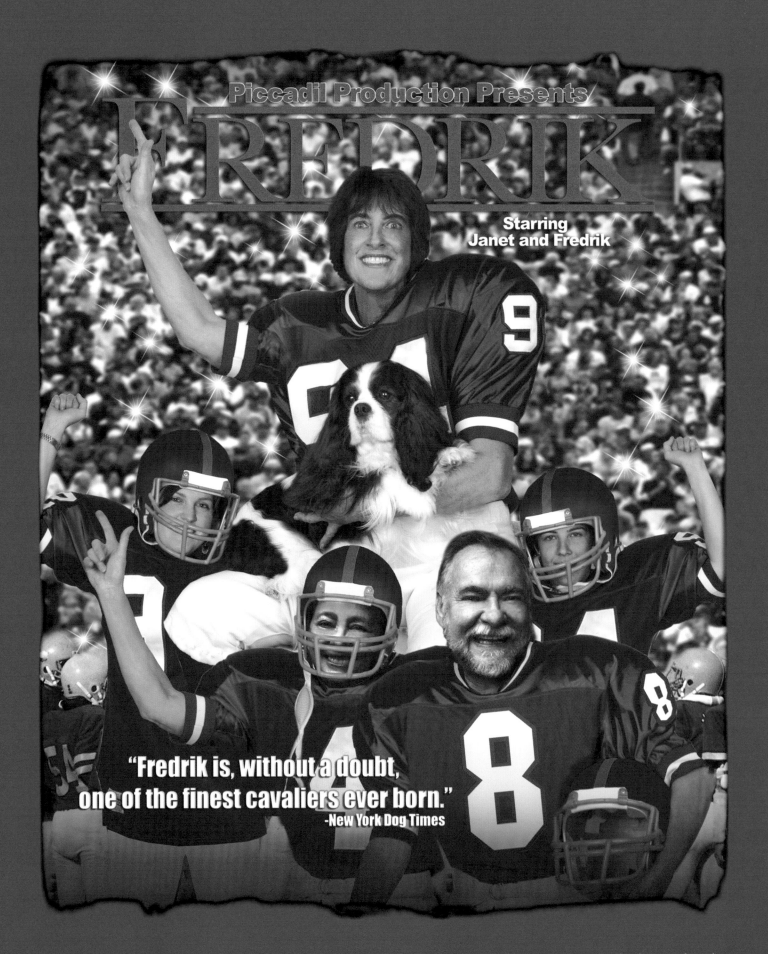

Piccadil Production Presents

FREDRIK

Starring
Janet and Fredrik

"Fredrik is, without a doubt,
one of the finest cavaliers ever born."
-New York Dog Times

Then, one evening in June, Fredrik saw *Rudy* on TV. The movie made him think. Had he given up too easily? Mr. Bigalow wasn't the only agent in Hollwood. Maybe he didn't even need an agent, but he needed to be in Hollywood.

He raced to the office and found Janet kneeling on the floor surrounded by brochures for summer dog shows.

"Are you feeling better, my Angel Boy?" she asked.
Fredrik answered with loving licks.
"I was just trying to figure out where we should go next," she said, as she scratched him under his chin.

Fredrik barked and pawed the flyer for a show in Pennsylvania and another in Ohio. He nosed brochures for shows in Illinois, Nebraska, Nevada, and California. Finally, he sat on one for a show in Beverly Hills, wagged his tail, and looked at Janet with his big, brown, melting eyes.
Janet laughed. "Are you trying to tell me something?"

So they packed their dreams—along with a two-month supply of liver biscotti and a few other essentials—and headed west. High on hope—with a list of the top ten animal agents in Hollywood—Fredrik, Janet, Paddy, Pippin, Nikkie, Cecile, Boogie, and Mondrian began their own glorious adventure.

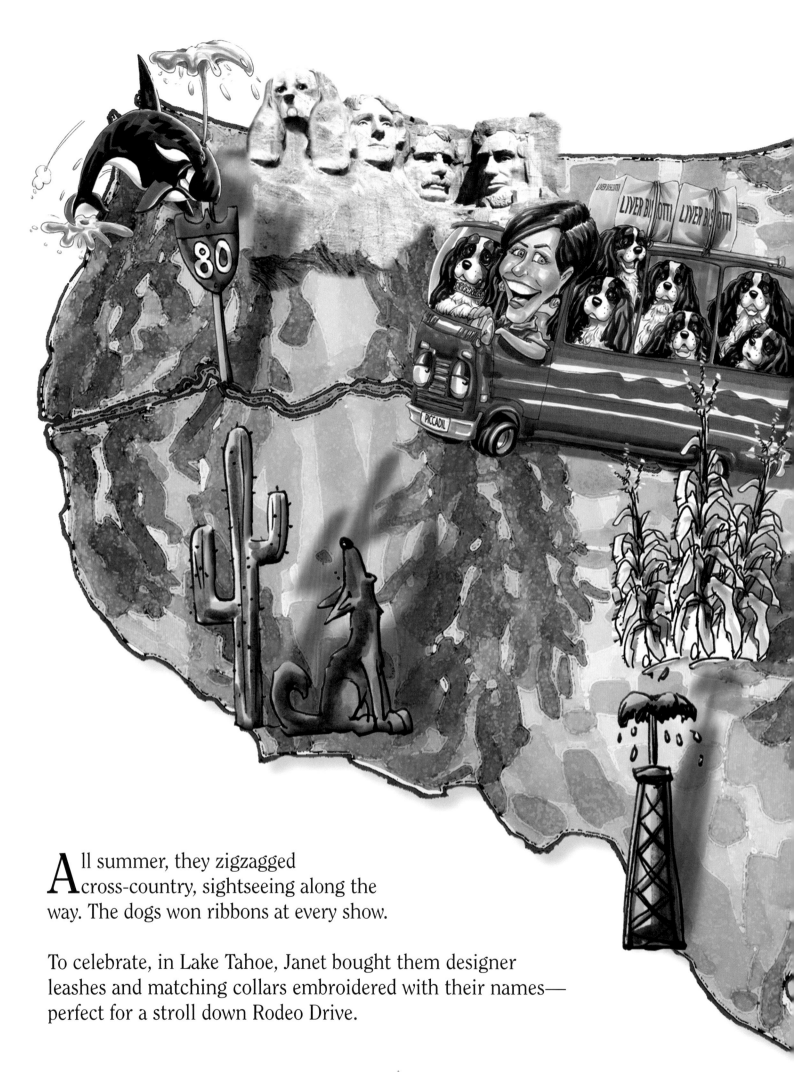

All summer, they zigzagged cross-country, sightseeing along the way. The dogs won ribbons at every show.

To celebrate, in Lake Tahoe, Janet bought them designer leashes and matching collars embroidered with their names—perfect for a stroll down Rodeo Drive.

Fredrik was excited the afternoon they left Nevada. By nightfall, they'd be in San Francisco; the next day, in LA. As they drove through the mountains and listened to CDs of movie themes, he pictured himself in films—*Saturday Night Fever,* *Star Wars,* and *March of the Penguins.*

GONE WITH THE WIND

Pennies from Heaven

"There's a world on both
sides of the rainbow"
But for Fredrik
"Everytime it rain, it rains
Best in Shows from Heaven!"

When *Tara's Theme* played, the skies
darkened and the wind picked up. As they
crossed the Nevada—California state line,
rain spattered against the windshield, and
the wipers beat to the rhythm of *Pennies
from Heaven*. The storm unleashed its
wrath, with visibility near zero Janet
looked for a place to pull off the road.

Fredrik trembled in the back of the van. Thunder terrified him. Janet spoke calmly, peering through the sheeting rain and holding the steering wheel in a white-knuckle grip. "It's all right, my Angel Boy. This will pass."

Without warning—or enough room—a tractor-trailer hauling new cars barreled into their lane. Janet blasted the horn and steered onto the shoulder. The van skidded, hit the end of the guardrail, and slid down the embankment. Glass shattered. Metal twisted. Airbags deployed. The kennels in the back bounced like tossed dice before the van came to rest at the bottom of the ravine.

Fredrik was the only dog not traveling in a kennel. He regained his footing and crawled to the front of the van.

He licked Janet's face and barked. She groaned, but didn't wake up. He howled until his throat ached. All the other dogs started barking, too, but no one came. He had to get help.

Fredrik squeezed out the broken window. He heard the rumble of engines, but he couldn't climb the steep, slippery slope to the road. Pelting rain drove him back into the forest. Lightning split the sky; thunder shook the ground. He dashed around boulders, over fallen trees, and across swollen streams for what seemed like hours. Distant sirens helped him find the interstate. Cars and trucks whizzed by without stopping.

He'd almost given up hope when a car pulled onto the shoulder. A girl peeked out the window. "I was right, Papa. It is a dog!"

As if to say, "Follow me!" Fredrik ran up to the car, barked, then dashed away. A man got out. "Here, boy. Don't be scared," he said. "We're just trying to help." Fredrik approached cautiously.

"That's a good dog. We won't hurt you." The man scooped Fredrik into his strong arms, handed him to the girl, and started the engine. Fredrik barked. He struggled to get out of the car. His nails clicked on the window as he jumped against the passenger-side door.

"Calm down," said the girl. "We'll take care of you." She wrapped him in a blanket. "Isn't he sweet?"

"Don't get attached," the man said, as he eased the car back onto the road. "You know Mama's allergic to dogs. We can't keep him. We'll take him to Silverwood. If we can't find his owner, we'll find him a good home."

"But, Papa...I really want a dog."

Fredrik started to tremble. He whimpered, then closed his eyes. What would happen to his family now?

He didn't remember falling asleep, but when he awoke, it was dark, and the car had stopped. The door swung open.
"How was your fishing trip?" said the woman.
"We didn't catch any trout," said the girl, "but we caught a dog."
"Oh, no!" said the woman. Aaaachoooo! Aaaachoooo! "Not a dog."

In the morning, a veterinarian in a mobile clinic pulled into Silverwood Winery. He examined Fredrik, pronounced him healthy, and scanned him for an ID.

"I can't find an implanted microchip," he told the vineyard manager, "but my scanner doesn't read international chips. He could be from a foreign country, but considering where you found him, I'll bet he's from Nevada. I've seen designer collars like these before. Pet boutiques in Lake Tahoe sell them. Maybe someone remembers embroidering one for Fredrik."

The vineyard manager called almost all the pet shops in Lake Tahoe without success. He intended to call the rest, but an unexpected visit from the winery's owner distracted him. Cameron Chandler Brewster—CC to family and friends—bought Silverwood ten years ago after his blockbuster film *Tidalwave* won six Performance Awards. The only child of legendary film star Kathryn Chandler, CC was a sucker for dogs. When he met Fredrik and discovered the adorable little spaniel needed a home, he offered to take him.

"My mother just moved into the guest house on my estate," CC told the vineyard manager. "She turns eighty this weekend. Fredrik will be an early birthday present. She's been sad lately. He'll cheer her up."

NAPA, CA

HOLLYWOOD

NAPA

FREDRIK

HOLLYWOOD, CA

They rode from Napa to Beverly Hills in a chauffeur-driven Rolls Royce. Kathryn Chandler fell in love with Fredrik the moment CC placed him in her arms. "I think this the beginning of a beautiful friendship," she said.

Fredrik liked Kathryn, too. She was kind and caring, and she rubbed his floppy ears just like Janet did. Thinking about Janet made him sad. He worried about her and missed his family.

Everyone who was anyone in Hollywood attended Kathryn Chandler's birthday gala. All cooed over the adorable dog in her arms. Guests toasted Kathryn's talent and beauty. Friends teased her about her age. When the caterer wheeled in her cake ablaze with eighty-one candles, Kathryn feigned fright and screamed, "Fire!"

Fredrik heard her scream, smelled the burning wax, and sensed Kathryn was in danger. He jumped onto the pastry cart and pushed the flaming cake into the swimming pool. It sunk with a sizzle. The guests gasped; Kathryn laughed.

"My hero!" she said, wiping frosting from Fredrik's nose.

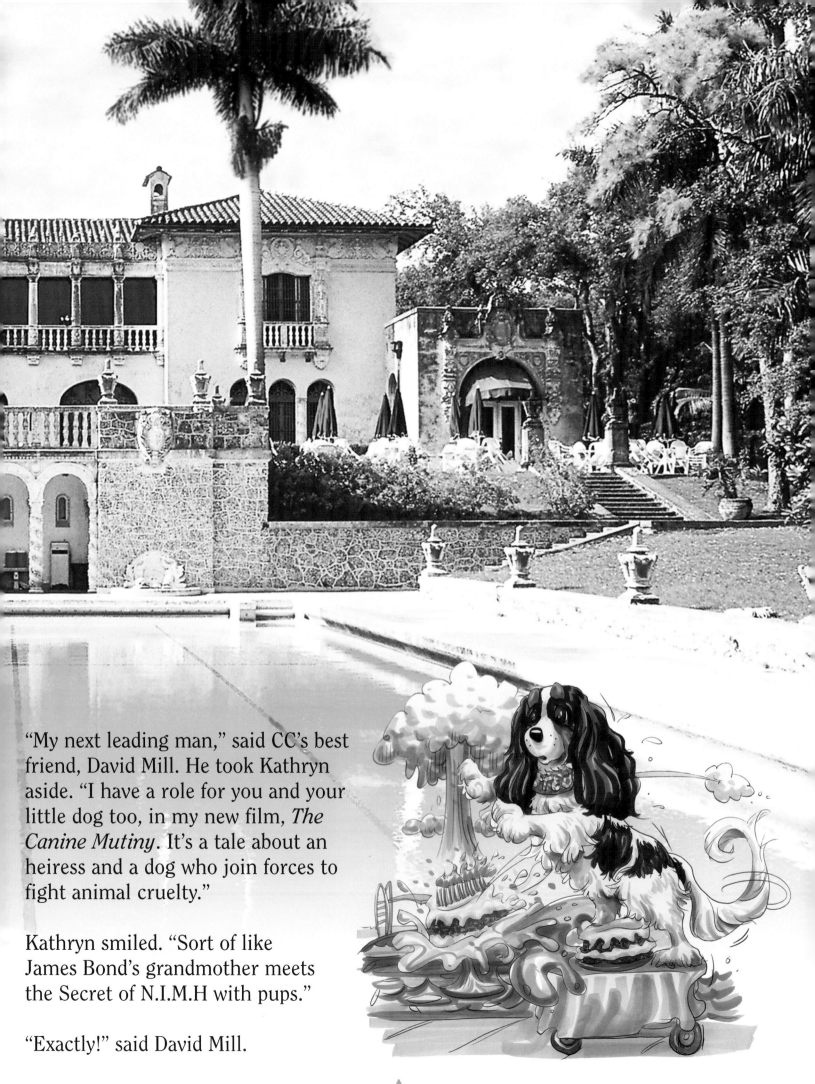

"My next leading man," said CC's best friend, David Mill. He took Kathryn aside. "I have a role for you and your little dog too, in my new film, *The Canine Mutiny*. It's a tale about an heiress and a dog who join forces to fight animal cruelty."

Kathryn smiled. "Sort of like James Bond's grandmother meets the Secret of N.I.M.H with pups."

"Exactly!" said David Mill.

By the end of the week, he had Fredrik's paw print on a contract.

Filming began in September on World Studio's back lot, where winter follows spring, New York is next to London, and the past and future live in the present.

For Kathryn Chandler, it was like coming home. For Fredrik, it was a new adventure—one he was supposed to have with Janet and Paddy, Pippin, Nikkie, Cecile, Boogie, Mondrian, and the other Cavaliers. They were always in his thoughts and heart. Were they safe? Together? Looking for him? Sometimes when he and Kathryn shopped in Beverly Hills, he'd catch a glance of a tall elegant lady and think it was Janet. He'd sensed his family's presence in other places, too—outside Hollywood's Rose Garden Café and in the Beverly Hills Pet Boutique where Kathryn bought him beef biscotti.

Now as he waited for the first day's shoot to begin, the same feeling crept over him. Maybe the replicas of the Bow Bridge and the Bethesda Fountain reminded him of their special walks in Central Park. Maybe it was wishful thinking, but on his way to the set that morning, he thought he'd heard familiar barks.

The snap of the scene marker broke his reverie.
"Canine Mutiny, Act I, Scene II, Central Park Dog Napping: Cue the Cavalier...and action!" They filmed take after take, but the shoot went well.

It was late when the limo dropped them back home. Kathryn changed into a flowing dressing gown, settled Fredrik on her lap, then picked up the phone and pressed the call button for the main house.

"Is CC there?" she said, as she rubbed Fredrik's ears. "No, just tell him I called."

She yawned and clicked on the TV. "I don't know what I want more—food or sleep." The celebrity chef on the Food Channel fixed a frittata. "Food!" she said, sliding Fredrik from her lap. He followed her into the kitchen. He'd been ready for dinner hours ago.

As Fredrik savored his sautéed liver, Kathryn poured olive oil into the frying pan and turned on the gas. While it heated, she whisked two eggs in a mixing bowl. "We've had quite a day, haven't we, my pet? When the cameras started rolling, I felt like shouting, 'I'm back!' How I've missed making movies."

Holding the carton of eggs, she turned to the refrigerator, but her heal caught on the hem of her dressing gown. She stumbled and fell. Fredrik rushed to her side, skidding on the gooey mess. He nuzzled her neck and licked her face. She moaned. He barked in her ear. She didn't move. He howled. No one came.

The oil in the pan burst into flames. Paper towels near the burner caught fire, and the flaming mass sparked the curtains. The smoke detector blared. Fredrik raced around the house. He had to get help. He wouldn't fail again.

The phone rang. Fredrik ran into the living room, jumped on the chair, knocked the handset off the receiver, and howled—long, mournful howls.

CC burst through the door moments before the firefighters arrived and carried his mother, awake and protesting, to the living room sofa. The firefighters quickly doused the flames; the EMTs *(Emergency Medical Technicians)* declared Kathryn bruised not broken. They wanted to take her to the hospital, but she refused. She said the blossoming bump on her head would save time in makeup.

"Tomorrow," she told the EMTs, "I play a jailed animal rights protester." During the chaos, paparazzi who monitor emergency broadcasts snuck past security and snapped pictures.

The next day's headlines read: *Spectacular Spaniel Rescues Silver Screen Star* and *Canine Hero Howls for Help*.

During the morning shoot, word of Fredrik's heroism spread through World Studios like wildfire. Kathryn basked in the attention; Fredrik ignored it. He thought only of the rescue that failed. He missed Janet and Paddy, Pippin, Nikkie, Cecile, Boogie, Mondrian, and the other dogs now more than ever. He'd never stop looking for them. Had they stopped looking for him?

At lunchtime, when Kathryn headed to the commissary with David Mill, her assistant took Fredrik for a walk. Going a roundabout way from Stage #24 to Kathryn's trailer, they passed several blocked-off streets. The assistant paused by a barrier. Fredrik saw horses pulling a hay wagon clip clop down a cobblestone lane.

"What are they filming?" the assistant asked.

"The Glorious Adventure," said the security guard, as he looked up at the overcast sky. But if it rains, they'll have to postpone the shoot."

Fredrik sniffed the air and caught a smoky scent—not melting wax or flaming oil, but a comforting smell like smoldering logs in the fireplace at home. He tugged free.

With leash trailing, he raced into 17th century London.

King Charles II scooped him up before he ruined the shot. Fredrik's heart raced. Familiar scents swirled around the man.

"What are you doing here?" the actor said. "We've finished all of our scenes. I thought you guys were leaving yesterday." He held Fredrik at arm's length. "Which one are you? Paddy? Pippin? Nikkie? Cecile? Boogie? Mondrian? You cuties all look alike. Where's Janet?"

Fredrik wiggled free. *They're here! They're here! He just knew it. But where?* He raced out of London and dashed through the streets of New York. It started to drizzle. He flew by the wardrobe building and the prop shop, the first aid station and the commissary. He darted between trailers.

The rain beat down hard and heavy. Where was his family? Desperate, he stood on his hind legs, pawed the air, and howled at the sky loud and long as if to yell: J-A-N-E-T! J-A-N-E-T!

The commissary doors flung open. "My Angel Boy! I've found you!" Fredrik leaped into Janet's arms and licked salty raindrops from her face. He was home. Janet carried him inside and a crowd engulfed them.

"This is Lisa Buttinski, host of *Hollywood Nightly*. I'm on the Red Carpet in front of the Kodak Theater with two-time Performance-Award winner Kathryn Chandler, award nominee—the chic, sleek, and unique Fredrik—and his beloved owner, Janet."

Buttinski thrust the microphone at Kathryn. "*Canine Mutiny* was a departure for you, but the gamble paid off. A *Best Actress* nomination for you, *Best Actor* for Fredrik. Do you think he has a chance against such Hollywood luminaries as George Tumey, Ben Queensly, and Denzel Jefferson?"

Kathryn smiled. "It's not about winning; it's about doing what you love. It's an honor just to be nominated."

Buttinski went on. "Were you devastated when you had to return Fredrik to his rightful owner?"

Kathryn draped her arm around Janet's shoulder. "I didn't believe her that day in the commissary when she told me Fredrik belonged to her. But who can argue with a microchip. Janet was so kind and understanding. We've become quite close. She stayed with us while we finished filming *Canine Mutiny.* And I've invited Janet and her Cavaliers to stay with me whenever Fredrik's in Hollywood." Kathryn turned to Janet. "Shall we give them an exclusive?"

Janet nodded. She looked radiant. "Fredrik's going to be a daddy! And I'm giving Kathryn one of his pups."

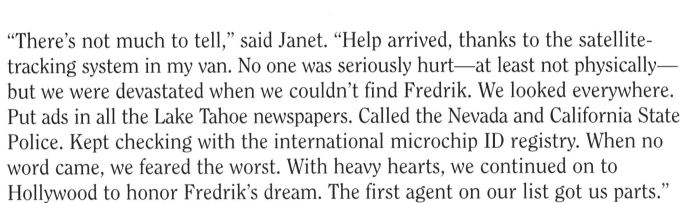

Buttinski thrust the microphone at Janet. "Fredrik's real-life story has all the drama and pathos of a four-star movie—a rescued dog, who depends on the kindness of strangers, becomes a rescuer himself. Fredrik has captured all our hearts. Please fill in the blanks for his fans. What happened after the car accident?"

"There's not much to tell," said Janet. "Help arrived, thanks to the satellite-tracking system in my van. No one was seriously hurt—at least not physically—but we were devastated when we couldn't find Fredrik. We looked everywhere. Put ads in all the Lake Tahoe newspapers. Called the Nevada and California State Police. Kept checking with the international microchip ID registry. When no word came, we feared the worst. With heavy hearts, we continued on to Hollywood to honor Fredrik's dream. The first agent on our list got us parts."

"And you and your dogs were cast in the *Glorious Adventure*, which is how you and Fredrik both ended up at World Studios," Buttinski added.

"Yes. I shudder to think how close Fredrik and I came to missing each other. I'd packed the van, and my Cavaliers and I were ready to head home when I saw the story in the morning paper. I just knew the "canine hero" was my Fredrik. I rushed to World Studios, and the rest, as they say, is history."

"Tell us what's next for the dog that's been called *"The Most from Coast to Coast."*

Piccadil Production Presents
Janet and Fredrik
Starring in
Must Love Fredrik

Janet York and Fredrik
IN
HONEY, I
SHRUNK
THE PUPS

"We've had so many offers," Janet said. "David Mill sent us scripts for *Must Love Fredrik*,

PICCADIL PRODUCTION
PRESENTS

MY FAIR FREDRIK

Starring Janet and Fredrik

Fredrik and Janet are
big

Honey, I Shrunk The Pups, My Fair Fredrik, and *Big,* so we'll have to get back to you on that."

The *Hollywood Nightly* host patted Fredrik's head. "Janet, you and Fredrik have had an incredible journey! Care to share what you learned along the way?"

"Life's like an agility course," Janet said. "Stay focused, take it one obstacle at a time, and don't give up. With hard work, perseverance, and a little luck, dreams really do come true."

"Kathryn," said Buttinski. "One final question for you. If Fredrik could talk, what do you think he'd say right now?"

Kathryn looked at CC and David Mill who had just joined them on the Red Carpet. "I can answer that," said the *Canine Mutiny's* director, as he ushered their group into the Kodak Theater. "He'd say…

'All right, Mr. D. Mill, I'm ready for my close-up.'"

The End

Acknowledgements

My sincere appreciation goes to:

Tom and Sande Weigand and Melanie Hess for their expertise in seeing that all the photographs in this book are perfect.

Jan Stitzel, a special thank you for her creativity and tireless work in providing these photographs.

Mike McCartney for his wonderful illustrations that capture the true personality of each of my Cavaliers and my one Chinese Crested.

Ellen Braaf for her excellent help and true interest in bringing this story to paper.

Julie Moser for combining photographs, illustrations and print matter together to create this unique storybook for children and adults alike.

And most important a big hug and squeeze to Fredrik, my darling Cavalier, who worked so hard and lovingly to please me and, now, all of you who read this book.

It is the intention of this author to encourage responsible ownership of Cavalier King Charles Spaniels. Your pet will be dependent upon you for its lifetime of up to 15 years. If you are interested in acquiring a Cavalier, or any dog, we suggest that you locate a responsible breeder who sells dogs in good health and of good quality.

For more information about Cavalier King Charles Spaniels or to locate breeders, contact:

The American Kennel Club
5580 Centerview Drive, Raleigh, NC 27606-3390
(919) 233-9767 www.akc.org

American Cavalier King Charles Spaniel Club, Inc.
Breed Information Services
www.ackcsc.org

Cavalier King Charles Spaniel Club USA, Inc.
Breed Information Services
www.ckcsc.org

Published in the United States by Piccadil Productions LLC
155 East 72nd Street, New York, NY 10021-4371
Email: Piccadiljy@aol.com
Printed in USA by N.E.W. Printing
First Edition, 2007
ISBN 0-9788314-0-3